TELL GOD I DON'T EXIST

UnderratedAnimalsPress

TELL
GOD
I

timmy reed

DON'T
EXIST

TELL GOD I DON"T EXIST

Originally published by **UnderratedAnimalsPress,** 2013

ISBN-10: 0989239004
ISBN-13: 978-0-9892390-0-4

UnderratedAnimalsPress
5708 N. Charles Street
Baltimore, Maryland 21210

underratedanimals.wordpress.com

Cover painting and text designed by
Timmy Reed

Author photograph by Carabella Sands

Don't Be Scared
It's Just Life

Stories

To all the lovely people in my life who make each trip around the ball of fire something to be grateful for: Thanks, guys.

The Earth Was a Living Thing

The earth was a living thing, like any of us. It breathed.

The entire planet was covered in skin. Countries were drawn around tan lines and bruises. Blemishes were mined for oil, which was burned for cooking and rituals. Our fires left bubbles and smooth pink wounds in the ground beneath us. We massaged them with jelly and wax. We built fences around abscesses, pits, eruptions. We erected monoliths of keratin and salt. We navigated soft pustules of all colors, dined on stalk of hair and flake of skin. Pores became our shelters, our home. We hunkered down as rank gasses rumbled within or pushed loudly out through the many scattered anuses that pocked this ball of flesh we lived on.

We slept through the day under the black sun, our bodies wet and salty with the sweat of the earth. It was all we knew, though we suspected there were other planets, planets constructed of other materials, older planets, planets where life meant something different than it meant here.

At night we emerged to practice our religion, the religion we had created for ourselves. The religion did not produce an explanation or provide answers, only questions and doubt. The doubts were shouted outward into the empty light of space and inward down cavities or muffled to paste as we pressed our faces hard against the spongy skin. Doubts were our only comfort, all of us tiny and terrified of what we might already know. Doubts were our version of faith, a way of supposing a meaning for life or pretending we might not all die completely, even the earth that held us.

Wet Sugar

Our neighborhood was expecting a storm.

We lived in a valley between two hills with a brown stream that hooked at the bottom, cutting us off from the rest of town. On one of the hills was a telephone tower. Below, there were houses and a tavern and store. There were also churches and a burial mound. Children played on the mound. Adults stayed away unless they had someone to put inside. The neighborhood was dense with priests and old women who had settled close, toes clenched, to watch each other.

In the few weeks before the storm, priests walked in silent lines through the streets. Women hid inside houses and sheds, making pies.

The children fed black birds that gathered on the mound. The birds ate bits of meat from their fingers.

The tavern was open to everyone, but always full of men. The men's backs curved like hooks as they leaned over the bar and talked into their drinks. The older men in the neighborhood developed bent shoulders with lumps that resembled the mound.

In the evening, candles were put outside of houses here and there throughout the neighborhood. Candles in front of priests' homes were prayers. Candles in front other homes were spells or placed there to light the way for children and husbands so they would come back at night to be warm.

I was the only child who stayed away from the mound, whether there was a funeral or not. I had no friends because of this. I wandered the streets and alleys with my little sister, Ruth, who pitied me. I made her hold my hand sometimes. I pretended it was for her sake. She pretended too. Ruth only avoided the mound when she was with me, but it felt like we were always together.

Some nights our mother left candles for us or for our father. Our father was inside the mound.

Ruth collected candy in hordes and tucked it away in invisible places. Worried mothers left out sweets for the children, hidden around doorsteps or tucked into gardens and under lawn ornaments. Ruth saved them for what she called "Emergency Special Occasions." I collected nothing but my own thoughts. I couldn't help myself. Even bad thoughts. I replayed my life in my head all day long, until I went to sleep at night. I forgot things anyway. Mostly good things, I bet.

I replayed the events of the storm in my head even though they hadn't happened yet.

Neighbors grumbled about who predicted the storm first. The only thing we all agreed on was that we could feel the air changing and it was best not to talk about, or to talk about very quietly.

Ruth and I walked everywhere together. People saw us so much that the whole neighborhood thought we were spying on them. Ruth didn't mind. She would have suffered any reputation to make me feel comfortable.

There was a tension in the air like static. The telephone tower hummed. Matches were more easily lit here than in other places. The air sizzled and tasted like copper buttons. Our mother lived her whole life in a nervous daze, as if she had just been slapped while alone in an empty room and was trying to ignore the presence of ghosts. She pretended life was not beautiful, but pretty. She kept plastic flowers in water until mold grew on the stems. She raised us like dolls from an old play set, I thought. She held us up to her heart sometimes and other times it was like we weren't there at all.

I knew the neighborhood and maybe even the world beyond it was beautiful. Anything beautiful was also terrifying. The hole in our family was at the top of that list.

I think Ruth had yet to find any of that out. She just nodded and pet my hand when I told her what I suspected about life. We both worried about our mother but I think I worried more because Ruth was so busy worrying about me.

The storm was about a week away. I heard men whisper or laugh through the opening and closing tavern door while I played pinball in the mudroom out front with Ruth at my side. The men never mentioned the storm directly. They wanted sandbags and batteries, the prayers of the faithful or a new girlfriend, without saying why they needed these things. I heard a story from the mouths of other children who were walking through my alley on the way to the mound. They said somebody was building a boat. They said they were building it to save all the bones.

My mother stood in the window and watched the mound. There was a row of houses between her and the mound so she couldn't see it with her eyes. She stared straight through the houses as if they didn't exist. Ruth and I coughed when we entered the kitchen. We walked with heavy feet so she would know we were home.

"Hello, children," she said. Or something very close. Her eyes were big and watery. She was holding a pair of large scissors. Lately it seemed like she was always holding something sharp when we came home. I looked around the kitchen for scraps. She had not been cutting anything. I put my hand on Ruth's shoulder.

"Hello, Mom," we said. Or something very close.

Ruth offered her a piece of licorice. She looked at the candy noodle as if it was a worm. Then she bit into it and chewed. "There's a storm coming," she said, with a shiver.

"We know," Ruth said and pulled me upstairs.

I was young when my father died and the memories I had of him were like a faded recording, worn thin and crackly and full of empty spots. Ruth was a baby when he died. I imagined her memory of him to be like a tinny song winding down on a music box. I couldn't imagine how my mother remembered him. It was probably a symphony.

We locked ourselves in my closet with a flashlight and cookies. The coats and sweaters were a wall of soft vegetation. "I'm scared for Mom," I whispered.

"Did you say 'of' or 'for'?" Ruth asked. "We don't need to whisper. We can just talk normally."

She was waiting for me to tell her "Both." I didn't need to. The fact that she was waiting meant she already knew.

"I think she's scared of the storm," Ruth said after a while. "People act weird when they are scared." She gave me a look. "You should know."

I didn't say anything. I ate a cookie.

"Maybe part of her wants the storm, too," she said.

I swallowed. "Why would anyone want a storm?" I asked. I had been trying to figure this out for a while.

"I don't know."

We sat in silence for a long time and ate cookies.

"I guess people get sick of waiting for things," Ruth said.

We made shadow puppets on the wall of the closet. Ruth created black birds with her little hands. I made a lonely dog. When I fell asleep her birds were still circling the closet, like they were trapped.

For a week it drizzled nonstop. A light grey mist filled the streets. Candles were still put out at night, under awnings or shielded by lampshades. Birds flew through the sky. The other children still played on the mound. They stared outward in a circle, waiting for someone to come for the dead. I watched two old women wrapped up in black scarves mumble back and forth through a knothole in their fence as they tended to their gardens. I made Ruth stop and stand still to listen. One of them said something about "wicked duration, not ferocity." The other made a noise like a squirrel.

There was a group of priests on a corner of the main drag through our neighborhood, the road that led to the mound. They were in long black or grey coats and huddled very close together as if to hide from the cold. They were all very tall and thin and their hats made them look taller, like giants. Even in their silence, I got the idea they were trying to remind us of something. Their presence on the street was a warning. I thought if they did talk, icicles would come out of their mouths. I stopped to watch for a moment, then walked past like everyone else.

I thought of Mom at home alone, waiting for the storm. She didn't need to be reminded of anything.

That morning she talked about what it must be like to drown. "Suffocating," she said a few times over breakfast, "Suffocation." She said she dreamt about being smothered as a little girl. In her dream she was choked by wet cloth, like her blankets were sweating on her. It was cold. She looked at the ceiling fan and took a breath.

Then she gave us a lesson in how to breathe. "In through the nose," she said. "Out through the mouth. It keeps your heart beating regular."

She asked if there were a death we would prefer to drowning.

"Death by chocolate," Ruth said.

The rains picked up over the weekend. On the radio there was talk of mud sliding down the hills and covering our neighborhood, turning it into a giant mound. The stream was swollen and rushing. It carried broken limbs and bits of trash. I had already been out for a walk. Some houses were sandbagged and boarded up, while other houses, like ours, had done nothing at all to prepare. The other children were circled on the crest of the mound, looking outward.

The tavern was packed. I suggested our mother go there to wait through the storm with our neighbors. I was always trying to get her out of the house to meet people, even if she already knew them. I wanted my mother to be happy because I thought if she were happy, I would be too.

Mom didn't respond to my suggestion. She walked over to the window and looked toward the mound. She picked up a knife and ran her finger along the serrated blade. It was the knife we used to cut bones when we needed to make stock.

Ruth asked me to take her out for another walk. We sprinted from tree to tree for cover. Ruth seemed to know where she was headed. I didn't care. I just didn't want to be at home. I didn't want our mother to be alone either. I didn't want anyone to be alone or get hurt or feel bad. More than that, I didn't want to think about those things anymore. I imagined crawling underground to sleep for a long time, hundreds of years, and yawning when somebody found me.

I thought about our house being washed away as I ran and the more I thought about it, the more I liked the idea. I thought about moving somewhere else, but I knew my Mom would not leave the neighborhood unless the mound was washed away too. It felt like we had all forgotten you could leave.

If the mound washed away, would our ghosts be free to follow us?

The streets would be littered with bones either way.

Ruth was too fast for me, even though her legs were smaller. I caught up with her under a weeping willow tree. It didn't provide much protection, but enough for us to talk. Lightning lit up the clouds and made them look like floating brains, sparked with electricity. Ruth was smiling. I was not.

"Where are we going?" I asked.

"Behind the store," she said.

I just looked at her.

"I have candy there," she said.

I wondered why she would keep candy behind the store and not in the house. I wondered why I didn't know any of this about her.

"It's not like we're joined at the wrist," she said.

"I know that," I said. I hadn't though. Not really. It was like I had been learning to pedal a bike and I just found out there was no one in back holding me up. I felt alone, but okay.

Ruth had already taken off running. I followed behind.

The store was catty-corner to the tavern. Both were full of people. I watched the customers in the store window as they rushed to wait in line, green baskets all stocked up with boxes and cans and batteries. There was a man outside under a tent selling ice. Across the street at the tavern people were smoking cigarettes out of cracked windows, huddled close to watch the lightning. The churches at the far end of the street were all lit up but empty. Ruth and I scurried down the middle of the road in our raincoats. We cut into an alley behind the store. The wind was picking up. I worried about the kids on the mound. I hoped they would go home to get warm. I did not think a boat was coming.

There was a pile of tires by the loading dock in back of the store. I had never noticed it before. The pile was covered with a coal blue tarp. Ruth pulled me under the tarp, which was being lifted at the corners by wind. She pointed at a crack between the tires. We peered through. There were huge black trash bags sealed with zip-ties, smooshed together and piled heavy inside like limp bodies.

"That's our candy," Ruth yelled through the rain.

She looked at me with hope when she said *our*.

"I need your help to move the tires," she said. "Because I'm too small."

I didn't understand how her tiny body could have gotten so much candy inside there. I asked her why she kept her candy in the tires.

"For emergency special occasions," she said.

"But why not keep it at the house where it will stay dry?"

"Because it's delicious." Even yelling, her voice sounded matter of fact. "I would eat it all."

We removed the tires and got dirty doing it. Ruth had black smudges on her cheeks. The wind ripped the tarp off the stacks. It flew through the air like a kite. The tires fell toward Ruth. I got in the way and the wet rubber knocked me down. I pushed the tires away. Ruth was smiling at me in the mud. She helped me up. I told her to stand by the loading dock. I got back to work.

Soon we stood in the growing rain with five giant trash bags that weighed more than both of us combined.

"Let's go," Ruth said. She grabbed my hand.

We loaded three bags on my back. Ruth put one over her shoulder and one we shared between us. We plodded down the center of the street side-by-side, trying to keep each other's pace.

Water was collecting along the sides of the roads.

I glanced at the mound as we moved past. Under a flash of lightning, I could see the black shapes of children scattering. Ruth led us down an alley and over two yards, until we were across the street from our home. The bags of candy felt like they were full of packed mud. The rain started to sound angry as we came inside.

Our mother was watching out the kitchen window. Our bags made a mess on the floor. Ruth began to light candles even though the lights hadn't gone out yet. She brought us into the living room, in front of the arched doorway, and sat us in a triangle. Mom carried a pair of scissors, which she held in her lap. The wet trash bags slumped on the outside of our triangle. They leaked sludge on the edges of the Oriental rug. I tried to hide a black puddle by sitting on it. Ruth pushed me away. She was over hiding things, I think. Mom didn't seem upset about the mess. She seemed like someone who was being swept off her feet.

Wind shook the bushes outside. Rain fell harder.

Mom and I sat quietly on the carpet as Ruth went upstairs and came back down with blankets and sleeping bags. We were unsure what to talk about. The weather was too obvious. We said, "I love you." It worked to fill the space between us. Then she held me and said, "Let's stay warm."

Ruth was still out of breath from our mission in the rain. She plummeted down the wooden stairs in a huff, riding on the blankets. There was nothing in her little pink face except a desire to make us comfortable. I got up to help her. I think Mom was going to also, but Ruth plowed over the hardwood too quickly for us. She was like an ant carrying dead beetles. We made a nest of pillows and sweets.

Two of the trash bags were filled with assorted candies: gum, toffee, jawbreakers, chocolates, and everything else we could imagine. The wrappers sparkled like glass. The other three bags were full of red shoestring licorice. Ruth encouraged us to eat all the candies, but she kept the licorice to herself.

A lot of the candy had gotten wet. It was sticky.

"Candy is good," Ruth said with her mouth full. She kept nodding. You could tell she thought we needed convincing. She weaved strings of licorice together as she spoke. "Let's just eat candy and be happy together," she said, chewing. "Let's just do that, okay?"

We ate candy for a day and a half. We ate it by candlelight after our power went out. The storm cooped us together. It made us feel close and crazy. We spoke to each other in made up voices. We stretched toffee between our teeth until we fell back and our heads hit the floor. We laughed at thunder. We sang. Our bellies ached, but we kept eating.

Ruth told us stories in which the three of us were characters. They were wild fictional stories where anything could happen. In one of the stories, we floated up to heaven and had a picnic. Heaven was not how I imagined it. It was more like real life, but people had forgotten to be unhappy. Our father was there. Ruth described him as if she had known him for eternity. I have never seen my mother so attentive. She played along, adding touches to the story; things like broken glasses and a cowlick and lost keys. She squeezed the scissors by the handles like she was holding a stuffed animal. She clapped and left the shears on the carpet, as though she'd forgotten they existed. She held my hand and squeezed. I held on too. It felt like I was taking a warm bath.

I noticed chipped fragments of rock candy stuck to my mother's cheek. I picked them off and ate them.

As Ruth narrated, she weaved more and more licorice until there was a very large red sheet braiding out in loose folds from her lap. It flooded our living room and out into the hallway. The whole house smelled like sugar and artificial strawberries and candles. Our mother sniffed deep, like she was in a garden. I wondered if Ruth was making us another blanket, or maybe a flag. I wanted her to tell me on her own, as part of a story maybe, so I didn't ask.

It turned out she was making a sail.

Water into Dust

I'm not sure what to think of my probation officer. Maybe I'm not sure what to think of anything. For instance, my P.O.'s last name is HURTTT. That's right, in all caps, with three T's on the end. I wonder if she's trying to make a point. She is eleven feet tall, a status I would classify as no less than Giant. Or Giantess, to be specific. She lives in a cave behind the county jail. The jail is fairly new and air conditioned inside. Her cave is not. There is, however, a fan. It blows a gentle whisper through the cavern, tickling Ms. HURTTT's diplomas off the wall, like water through the gills of a shark. Ms. HURTTT drinks wine in front of me despite my condition. She slurps it out of a human skull I suspect of belonging to her predecessor. She also collects gold. Coins, bars and trinkets that gleam in stacks around her desk along with all her needlepoint mottos, collectible coozies, and rubber-plastic trolls. The trolls are static-haired and naked. They watch me with google-eyes as I give urine specimens behind the bookshelf, which is full of stolen comics.

When Ms. HURTTT speaks, the torches often flicker. I can't ever recall precisely what she has been telling me. Only an ominous impression, something vague and dark. I've heard from certain judges that hers is the only proper treatment program for all of us poor bastards. That or jail, where it's air-conditioned and there aren't any trolls. I'm never sure what to think. Some of the other names on Ms. HURTTT's sign-in sheet are made of hieroglyphs. I sign in print and feel lonely. I have fevers. I cling to her stockings like a squirrel caught on the roof during a nasty tempest. Her calves are itchy with either leg hairs or parasites. I'm never sure of anything. I can see my reflection in her lip-gloss, I think. On my way home each Tuesday and Thursday, I drag my toes along deep grooves in the path that leads from her office. And cry. My tears turn to dust on the ground. I accept the things I cannot change and thank God for creating them.

Animal Hospitality

Yesterday it was cold out, the coldest day of winter, and the city invited all the bums inside and I felt bad for the squirrels because my hair is much longer than a squirrel's and I was inside and I know I was still a little bit cold. So I thought about letting them all come inside to get warm.

And I did.

I made a fire in both fireplaces and turned up the heaters full blast after my parents left for work, and I baited them with an array of baskets filled with nuts and dried fruits and cheeses and candy that were left over from Christmas last week when my parents' clients like to say thank you, sending lots of these things. With all the exits open to the bitter air, I hunkered down under a sleeping bag and waited, watching TV and munching a chocolate reindeer.

And they came.

They came, o boy did they come. A lot, like thirteen or something.

But it was cool for a while, like a couple of hours. Then it got old.

And even though today is truly frigid, colder than yesterday maybe, I think they should leave. The initial effect has worn off. They're more than cramping my style. But the squirrels won't leave, and other animals have started coming in too. I caught the neighbor's dog in the kitchen, for instance, and last night I heard what sounded like a couple of crows in my older sister's bedroom.

There's frost everywhere and my parents have left me. They say they are staying at a hotel until I go back to college. Basically it has come down to this: Just us. Me and the animals.

In desperation, I sit down in front of the television to pray, in Latin: "Pater Noster, que es in caelis..." The noises in the house are varied, made up of my own mumbling, the rodent chatter of the creatures around me, gusty winds, and the sound of the television, the Travel Channel, a show about the La Brea tar pits, all the way on Wilshire Boulevard in Los Angeles, where the scene is sunny and well-lit, but with a definite creeping overcast. I'm praying, but I'm still watching, wrapped up in blankets and surrounded by the elements, which have completely taken over, and the tar pits have been found to contain over one million fossilized skeleton parts, including mammoth, sabre-tooth cats, ground sloth, and mastodons, which reminds me of fields trips to DC as a kid and the dinosaur bones I used to see there. They were huge and white and authentic. They loomed over me, proof of something too big to imagine.

A chipmunk bumps my foot, apparently confused by the patterns on the carpet, and I stop praying, suddenly embarrassed.

I remember asking my mother about God's bones after one trip to the museum. She laughed and said He didn't have any. I was suspicious of course. I'd seen a *dinosaur* that afternoon. If He exists, shouldn't He have bones or something?

Those bones, gigantic, too big to be looked at, were terrible and uncanny to consider and they gave me nightmares, like a vampire movie or a frightening deformity I'd seen once on the street that made me hide in my mother's jacket.

Freezing, I pull the blankets tighter, and shut my eyes. The animals are laughing at me and the wind howls.

Reward

The quest started with signage: Reward, Missing Tortoise. The torn page was attached to a lightpost with a strip of clear tape filled with bubbles that brought oceans to mind, a blanket of surf. I had to find this lost creature, a prehistoric remnant at large in the human city, just like me.

Birds

.

I live on the roof of a building. The part of the roof I live on is surrounded by brick walls, so my only view is the sky. Bugs come visit me. They buzz my patio. They sneak inside and crawl on my lips when I'm sleeping. Birds don't come around much though. I have a little rooftop garden that might attract them, but all I grow is hot peppers. I suspect the birds somehow know to stay away from them. Or else they know to stay away from me because when I am out there, I am usually writing about you.

Occasionally I will be writing about you on my porch in the sun and I won't know what else there is to say, so I will look up at the sky. And I will see a bird. Actually, I will see the belly of a bird, flying overhead. In a second the bird will be gone and I will have to start thinking about you again.

Sometimes the birds are alarmingly big. I live in the city so mostly they are pigeons and the occasional seagull, but sometimes a hawk or a vulture will coast over my garden on very large wings and cast a bold shadow like a graffiti stencil on the tarpaper roof. I wish that these birds were even bigger, so large they filled the sky above my apartment and blocked out the sun when they flew by. I want a long gust of wind to blow the dead skin off my face. I want to look up from my writing and all I see is feathers. I want goose bumps when I write about you.

The Children Are Our Future

A young boy asked me, "What do the fishes drink?"

I mumbled something about the souls of inquisitive children, then pointed at a squirrel chewing on a battery.

"Where do batteries come from?"

I didn't know that one either.

"The supermarket," I said.

I pointed to a plastic bag caught on a tree branch. It flapped in the breeze like a flag.

"Where do plastic bags come from?"

"The supermarket," I said again. It felt good to know one for sure.

"Where do supermarkets come from?"

I said nothing. We kept walking, quiet until the boy stopped and pointed at my face.

"You forgot to finish shaving," he said.

Bioluminescence

Bioluminescence exists in the waters of almost every region of the globe, the tour guide told us. He stroked the bay and the mangroves around it with his laser. Then he repeated himself en español. But only in a very few special places are the micro-organisms responsible for this magical phenomenon able to survive in such numbers that one can see them clearly, illuminated bright enough to read a book by. The conditions generally required are: very salty waters, dense thickets of mangrove to act as a filter, a bay or lagoon, and darkness. "These are the conditions that provide the ideal environment for this type of bioluminescence," he said. "They are the same conditions that attract mermaids. Although we realize there are many mosquitos biting you, please refrain from using insect repellent as it is not good for the plankton." This too was repeated in Spanish.

Sometimes people, who always want proof of magic, take rum-soaked tours to visit the bioluminescence and swim in it.

I was with many other people on a pontoon boat. The sky was black and we had been drinking. Piña coladas or rum punch, depending on personal preference. Drinks were included in the price of the tour.

Everyone around me giggled while the tour guide pointed out the entrance to the bay and the planet Jupiter and Orion the Hunter. We knew we were about to see something magic. And swim in it.

I brushed against a young girl's arm and she jumped. She was that excited.

Usually I am not so excited to be led around by tour guides, but I could tell this glowing stuff was really going to be something special and I didn't want to miss it. Besides, they served drinks. I leaned over the railing of the boat and watched the wake glow a greenish-blue color as we approached an area of the bay that was thick with the plankton. The pontoon boat slowed and the anchor was dropped. We waited anxiously in line while we were given yellow flotation belts and led down a small ladder into the bay. I was at the back of the line. I could hear laughter and manic squeals each time someone entered the bay. I saw the glow of the tiny bubbles emanate from their extremities as they treaded water.

"Holy shit!" a woman screamed as she got to the bottom of the ladder and pushed off. "Watch me float in Magic Bay!"

Our giddy group of swimmers turned into children among the illuminated plankton, dancing and spinning and diving as deep as their belts would allow. They lifted their arms from the water and watched the green specks dribble off their wet skin like drops of Mercury. They spit water from their mouths. They splashed each other. They smiled. One young couple was making out in a wreath of non-thermal light.

Because of the festive nature of the scene, the air and the water and the rum and the glowing, anything was possible. People hollered at the sky like madmen. When the old woman yelled, "Oye! Dios mio!" I was not all that alarmed.

The mermaid floated in from the entrance of the bay on a pad of bioluminescence. The little glowing animals glistened in her long wet hair and on her skin. They dripped in squiggles off her belly. She was coughing and vomiting on herself.

Our party crowded around her, treading water. I was off to the side, hovering on the edge of the circle. From my perspective it appeared as if she were glowing herself, but a cool white glow, different than the plankton around her. Someone reached out and touched her shoulder. She flinched and spewed a stream of oyster and seaweed onto her chest. Bright green snot bubbled out her nose.

The guide and his apprentice grabbed a hold of her with a hook and dragged her toward the boat. The bioluminescence trailed behind her like pilot fish and dripped off her scales as they lifted her from the water. They lay her on a torn vinyl bench. The rest of us bobbed in silence at the edge of the boat, not sure whether the tour had ended. They held her hair back as the mermaid choked and spit saltwater into a bucket. She shivered and her teeth chattered so they wrapped her in a towel, which didn't seem to help much. When we finally got back on board, I snuck a peek in the bucket. The water inside was glowing.

I am inclined to describe this particular mermaid as very beautiful, but you could also tell she was very ill. Her face was pale and white like a pearl but she was turning blue around the gills, which the tour guide's apprentice kept rinsing with seawater. The guide tried his best to communicate, to figure out what was wrong, but the mermaid didn't have good English or Spanish. The conversation went nowhere. One man tried German, but that didn't work either. I hoped that maybe Latin might work and I could show off in front of everybody like Doctor Doolittle, but I hadn't really spoken it since high school (except in prayer) and I didn't want to embarrass myself in front of the mermaid or the other members of the party.

The mermaid looked as if her guts were being scraped clean from the inside, but none of us knew how to treat her. "Is there a doctor on the boat?" one man hollered. "Or a veterinarian?"

Our guide and his apprentice were marine biologists of sorts. They spoke in loud whispers, hissing at us to be quiet, to give the mermaid peace, we were scaring her. I made sure to follow their directions. She did look scared. Every flashlight or lantern on the vessel was pointed right at her, leaving the rest of us to mumble and stare in the darkness. I couldn't tell if she was crying or just wet. I know she had the hiccups. And her eyes were glazed over.

The mosquitoes were vicious out there on the Bahía Bioluminescente. We sat on wet benches, quietly dripping, and one girl tried to feed her crackers. She said that was what her mother did to her when she came home drunk from a party. Maybe the mermaid was drunk, she said. That seemed plausible to several of us, but not to everyone.

Maybe she is sick, a woman's voice said, with something contagious and we should put her back in the water.

Maybe she has old age, a little boy squeaked.

There were too many maybes, too many voices. The tour guide asked everyone to be quiet as he looked for a waterproof pen. When he found it, his apprentice began to take down notes for a vote.

The following is a list of ideas that came out of our discussion:

1. The mermaid needs to be taken to the hospital and then, once healed, given over to the proper Federal authorities. Everyone knows that the government has been trying to get their hands on a mermaid forever, for one reason or another.

2. She should be taken and put in an aquarium so the general public can be properly entertained by her physical oddities.

3. The mermaid ought to be delivered to the University. There are smart people there who will take this responsibility away from the tour group.

4. Take her back to the casino. She may be good luck.

5. The mermaid needs a change of diet. She needs to eat more fruits and vegetables. She must remove shellfish entirely.

6. The tour group must collectively pray to Saint Adjutor, the patron saint of swimmers.

7. The tour group must try to learn her language. And speak it upon returning to the resort, like a secret code.

8. The mermaid must be pulled through the bay behind the boat. The wake rushing though her gills will revive her.

9. The tour group should sing to her. If she is dying, her death should be beautiful and meaningful and special like the bioluminescence tour is described in the brochure.

10. The world needs to know about this. Everyone should be filming it on their camera phones.

11. Feed her rum punch.

12. Leave her in her natural environment. She has come to Magic Bay to die and the tour group must not disturb the natural process.

13. Everyone hold hands.

We stood around in the darkness for a while interrupting each other. The mermaid sat wide-eyed, shivering in the spotlight. I had no idea what we should do with her, so I just kept my mouth shut. All I knew was that I wanted to kiss her. She was pretty in a sublime, fishy sort of way. If she were going to die, I wanted to be her last kiss. I got caught up in a fantasy where my kiss would cure her and she would flop off the deck of the boat and swim away, leaping like a dolphin as she passed through the entrance of the bay. But I didn't kiss her. I was too shy.

I dreamt of kissing her and everyone else argued and multiple votes and recounts were taken and the mermaid threw up again and nothing was decided. Jupiter kept on shining above us and the bioluminescence circled the boat like a wreath. The batteries on peoples' flashlights started to die one by one. Eventually we were in darkness. Everyone grew quiet. You could hear the mermaid's teeth chattering. Our bathing suits had long since dried out and we began to fall asleep. While we slept, we were eaten by mosquitoes. At one point I woke up and saw her, shivering and covered in vomit. Specks of bioluminescent dust sparkled in her hair. I watched her in the moonlight staring at Jupiter and I loved her and was scared of her at the same time. I wanted so much to hold her, touch her hair with my face. Then we made eye contact. I looked away and when I looked back, she was still staring at me. Her eyes were no longer glassy, but penetrating and I felt like she could read my mind, had been reading it all night maybe, watching my dreams as I slept. Then she opened her mouth and silently shaped her lips around one word, "Loser."

When we woke up in the daylight, the bioluminescence was invisible and the mermaid was gone. A blue puddle shimmered where she once sat. Everyone was yawning and stretching as the guide flicked on the engines.

We went back to the island and took a ferry to the larger island and then took a large van to the resort. The tour group was very quiet along the way. Everyone looked at their phones the whole time. The air felt like the inside of a wet sleeping bag. Someone passed around a bottle of aspirin. I shut my eyes and leaned my face against the window. There would be a rainforest tour that afternoon.

After the Storms

The tornado is still just standing there outside our doorway, waiting, even though we have headphones on and are pretending we're not home. The trees in our neighborhood danced all night in the rain, then stood naked and shivered as the sun grew in our side window this morning. Children run through the alley now, picking up sticks from across town. Five tornadoes touched down in the city last night but ours is the only one that stayed, wrapped tight in a swirl of grey like an ancient woman at our doorstep, begging for a home. We hunch on the carpet in silence and stare at the door. We are trying not to laugh.

Starfish

I would love it if I knew someone who was born holding hands with a starfish. Clutching a starfish against their tiny bosom. That would be the coolest person I know for sure. It would suck if that happened and they were a real asshole though. If you are born clutching a starfish to your tiny bosom, you ought to live up to that standard of coolness.

If you are a girl you should be tough and wise and beautiful and mysterious, the kind of girl that everybody wants to be close to but no one will ever fully understand. You should be an elusive creature, someone that leaves an impression with very few words. Haunting, even. But you should also be the kindest person that anyone can think of when the subject of kind people they know comes up. You should wear peculiar pieces of jewelry gracefully, each piece given to you by someone special that you never talk about. You should have a beautiful singing voice but never be heard singing. Very few people should actually know where you live. You should be someone who shows up at ten things every weekend but only stays for a few minutes at each. You should be the kind of lady who always appears to be glowing, but only when one gets a chance to see her.

If you are not a girl born clutching a starfish, but a boy instead, then you should be gentle and friendly and sweet and wise and you should also be mysterious. You should be named something plain but odd. You should probably be handsome, but charmingly imperfect in appearance. You should ride everywhere on a bicycle and rarely borrow anyone's car, except for solitary road trips to go camping or something like that. You should collect odd things that you find and never show to anyone unless they ask you specifically. You should live in a converted carriage house that is tucked away in some underdeveloped neighborhood and, obviously, you should live by yourself. No one should ever really have a full grasp on what it is that you do for a living, but you should never need to borrow money. Likewise, everyone should know that you are an artist but no one should be able to put their finger on exactly what kind of art it is that you make. You should be very good at whistling. You should be the kind of fellow that makes people feel like the world is all right after all, even if they have to find out later on that it is not.

Wouldn't it be nice to have a friend that was born holding a starfish? It would be a constant reminder that life is not as bad as it seems.

I wonder who the mother would be.

Stealing Tigers

Once it was late at night and I was alone so I sent my friend a text message that said: "Bored...Let's go rob a bank."

"Or steal a tiger!" was what she sent back. So we went to the zoo.

The zoo was a very dark place at night compared to the rest of the city and it was unusually cool for the time of year, which added to the scariness of the situation. We looked in through the tall iron gate and were nervous, but when we looked at each other we couldn't control ourselves. We were laughing our heads off. Once we settled down some, we climbed over. I was very surprised when we found ourselves on the other side in one piece. Neither of us had any idea how we were going to get the tiger back over the gate once we had gotten hold of him. We marched ahead, down a pedestrian avenue lined with cages, feeling goofy and grand.

The zoo seemed to be asleep at first. We figured most of the creatures had been put away for the night. Then we started to hear noises. Owls, my friend decided. I trusted her judgment, although they sounded more like ghosts to me.

We kept moving, past a darkened aviary and the leopard cage. The leopards were invisible if they were in their cages at all. We both wondered whether the tigers would be in their cages or tucked away on a shelf somewhere in the back.

"Do we have anything to drink?" she asked me.

"Yes!" I almost screamed when I felt a flask in my pocket. I had forgotten about it entirely. I was excited to be useful. I handed her the flask.

"Not for me, kiddo," she said. "For the tigers."

"Of course! I bet tigers get mighty thirsty!"

"They do."

The tiger cage was empty. At least it looked that way at first.

But then it wasn't empty. There was a big fucking tiger, right in front of us! He had just sort of materialized out of the darkness. It was almost like he wasn't real.

"Let's pet him first. Then we'll steal him."

I agreed.

But I wasn't sure how to go about doing any of it. There was a railing and a ditch like an empty moat, about five feet across. There was a sign over the ditch that warned of tiger urine being sprayed when the cats were in heat.

We passed the flask once and helped each other fumble across the divide, which was moist with what was presumably tiger urine. With her soggy shoes on my palms, I boosted my friend up to the cage where she knelt to pull me up by the wrist. Perched against a black iron rail and clinging to the bars, we peeked in at the tiger. He stared back at us. He was at the front of the cage now. He moved like a spirit, or smoke.

We looked at each other and grinned. We poked our hands into the cage. We had to reach over this bulletproof glass thing at the bottom of the cage. Why would anyone want to shoot a tiger? We only wanted to steal him. Then we'd probably set him free.

In a matter of seconds I had all these thoughts about the adventures he might have once he was a free tiger living on the streets of Baltimore: Maybe he would become a research scientist or an art student...or a policeman...or a postal worker carrying a bag of mail in his mouth. What neighborhood would he live in? What bars would he hang out at? Maybe he would develop a drug habit. I imagined a Bengal tiger nodding out on the bus stop near my house. I remember thinking what a beautiful sight that would be, although I'm not sure why. Drug addiction is a tragedy, I thought, especially when it happens to a tiger...Maybe he would get a gig as an arabber, slinking around next to a horse and cart full of produce, roaring at potential customers in rhyme. My thoughts were racing...

I felt something wet on my palm. It was his tongue. He was licking both of us at once. His tongue was that big. We opened the flask and she poured it over our hands. The tiger drank off them intently, his eyes closed and purring.

When the vodka was finished, the tiger took a step back and cocked his head at us. Then he yawned. His jaws were enormous and his teeth glowed in the darkness. Neither one of us could tell if he was drunk yet. I'm not sure that we brought enough liquor for that. It's hard to tell with tigers. He curled up and fell asleep at our feet. "I feel bad waking him," she whispered.

I agreed. He did look peaceful. We let him rest. Soon enough, we fell asleep too, leaning against each other on a nearby bench. And we dreamt of stolen tigers.

When we woke up it was light out and the zoo was about to open. The tiger was nowhere to be seen. It was like he had never existed at all. We waved goodbye to the cage and hid out by the petting zoo, where we met a goat named Annie. Or at least she was named Annie after we met her and gave her a name.

We never named the tiger though. Tigers shouldn't be given names.

I Will End and the Planet Will End
But I Will End First and
For That I am Jealous of The Earth

I enjoy life but know I cannot live forever and this makes me sad but also jealous and angry of entities (like the planet) that will get to experience more life than me. I wish I never thought about dying. It's never a good thing. For instance, I thought about dying before my nap this afternoon and I woke up with a sore throat and a deep ache in the right side of my chest. The ache is menacing. Of course I fear it is a tumor. The worst-case scenario is always the easiest to fear.

The planet Earth is not actually alive in a biological sense – although there are innumerable living things on it and inside of it; all the life we know in fact – so it doesn't have to worry about menacing things like cancer. Someday the Earth will come to its end. Just not for a long time after this tumor (or something else) has killed me.

People are always talking about saving the Earth. I like to imagine the Earth is listening. Listening and thinking: *You need to save yourselves, Living Things. I am not going anywhere until the sun explodes. Make life nice for yourself. I have given you a place to grow. I have allowed you to be my tenants. My parasites.*

I am jealous of the Earth not only for the life it will lead after I am buried in its flesh but also for the enormous life it got to experience before I existed. Countless reiterations of my own lifespan, of the oldest man's lifespan, of the lifespan of the oldest tree, of the lives of all men and all trees. The Earth has been around that long, never coming to an end. Think of all it has seen!

And felt: the constant tickle of life like fungus growing on its belly and reproducing, spreading and building and even trying to leave by blasting off in tiny rockets. I am jealous of the Earth. I am jealous in the way that one can only be jealous of something they love but will never understand.

In the future, after humans have destroyed themselves with atomic ray guns and fast food diets, the Earth will remain just as it remained when the dinosaurs died off watching the sky, gripped by the beauty of falling meteorites. None of the fossils that have been discovered indicate whether dinosaurs experienced jealousy or not, but I cannot blame them if they did.

The Earth has been hospitable to me, if indifferent to my brief existence. I think about living on the Earth and feel like I am visiting a large country estate with too many rooms, so many that no one is sure exactly who is staying over at any given moment. But the Earth is not an uninformed majordomo. The Earth is the estate itself. It doesn't know who is staying inside its walls or care whose name is on the deed claiming ownership. The estate doesn't know that anyone owns it at all.

It does not make sense for the Earth to be jealous of me. What would it be jealous with, not to mention of? It hasn't got a brain. Not having a brain, even for a short time like my lifespan or yours, one might think of as an upsetting handicap but I don't think that's how it works. The Earth is never upset. It cannot understand what it means to be upset. It spins satisfied through the eons in the dumb blackness of space. With no brain, it has no consciousness and with no consciousness it harbors no fear of death and with no fear of death it feels no sadness or anger or jealousy.

I dwell on these things as I surf the Internet, kind of searching for clinics that I can afford without health insurance. I need someone to look inside me. I need someone to tell me I am all right, that my end is a long way off. I need someone to tell me there is the slightest chance that it may never come at all.

Maybe I am not jealous of the planet's lifespan, it occurs to me. Maybe I am jealous that the Earth doesn't have to deal with being alive at all. And just like that, I am not jealous because I remember that I enjoy being alive. But only for a while. Later I will be jealous again. I always am.

Bomb the Moon

I watched on television the night the President bombed the moon to look for water. Part of me wanted the moon to bomb us back. I didn't want to see anyone hurt but I felt like we could use the distraction. We must be bored if some of us are shooting rockets at the moon and the rest of us are at home watching it on television.

The explosion of lunar sand was almost invisible, unless you were on the moon to watch it. The footage I saw had been magnified many times and still only looked like dandruff on a man's skull, a blip of static popping against the screen.

Some of the wet lunar sand had bad things in it, like mercury. The same way some of our water has bad things in it, like mercury or great white sharks.

I think about the thirsty children on the charity commercials on TV. The ones who are dying, the ones with the flies that leave larvae in their tear ducts so they can no longer cry. I wonder what they know about the water on the moon.

Do they ever stare in desperation when it's full? When it shrinks, do they see it as half-empty?

Rendezvous

Things occur to me from time to time. My brain works on its own. I'm not always telling it what to do. I'll be sitting outside the laundry with a cigarette and I will see two ants walking alongside a reservoir of grape soda that has filled a crack in the sidewalk.

They will stop to visit the lake and I will be watching them, not thinking anything at this point, until they turn their little bodies around and walk off in divergent paths. Then I will find myself wondering: Will they ever see each other again?

I'll want to know if the ants share my concern. Do they wonder if they'll ever see each other again? How far does an ant travel in its lifetime? It's hard. I think about how small an ant's legs are, how low the horizon appears to their eyes.

Moles

I like moles. Not the cosmetic imperfections, but the small subterranean mammals. In fact, I've written about them before. But there was a different protagonist in that story. This time it's actually me. In this story, I like moles.

One time I was staying at a cabin near a lake that belonged to my friend and her husband. I was staying there because life had gotten busy in the city I love and there was work stress and money trouble and the alcohol had come back and of course there was a girl. So I was hiding out at my friend's cabin. And there were moles there.

The moles lived in a lonely pile of earth across the yard from Betsy's garden, which was the site where her husband Rick had been going to build a swing set. But then there was the miscarriage so the swing set never got built and the mound just sat there, ignored. And they ended up with a molehill instead.

After about a week of moping around, not writing anything,

not doing much at all, I wandered out into the yard while everyone was at work. I found myself over near the mound, in a corner of the yard by the edge of the woods. It was shady there and looked sad. I climbed up and sat cross-legged on top.

I was sitting there only few minutes when I began to notice all these little holes everywhere I looked. They made me nervous at first. I thought of snakes and creepy things. I was very surprised when a little black face popped out right between my knees. It was a mole! I had never seen one so close up before...He looked like a worm, cylindrical and sort of slimy with traces of pink skin showing through his charcoal black coat. I liked him immediately. I was sure he would run off or scurry back down his hole, but he didn't. He just gazed up at me, past me, from under his blind, folded eyelids, apparently oblivious.

So I picked him up! And he let me!

We were friends. I could tell.

Then another one popped out of a little hole to my left. I picked him up too.

Now I was holding two moles!

And I liked it.

We sat like that for a while until it started to rain. I let the moles crawl back into the earth. I remained there for some time and got wet. Then I went back inside and decided I would learn about moles.

The Hairy-Tailed Mid-Atlantic Mole is slim in shape and dark in color. Its diet is largely made up of earthworms and insects, but it will occasionally dine on a small mouse if one of them is unfortunate enough to get near the entrance to a colony. The Hairy-Tailed Mole inhabits Virginia, West Virginia, Pennsylvania, and Western Maryland.

In the early days of Modern English, British moles were known as "mouldwarp "mould" meaning "soil" and "warp" meaning "throw." Male moles are called "boars" and female moles are called "sows." A group of moles is called a "labor."

For centuries, moles have been misunderstood animals. I related to that. Mainly the cause of this misunderstanding has been things like: contamination of silage with soil particles, pasture and yield reduction, damage to young plants from the disturbance of soil, and damage to agricultural machinery by the exposure of stones. I had a different set of issues of course, but still I could relate.

So I started spending more time with the moles. Making daily visits to their sad little mound. I met more and more of them. Some were bigger than others, but basically they all looked alike. I couldn't really tell them apart and when I tried to give them individual names, I ran into trouble. They would remain a labor of nameless moles.

I had zero idea what their total population amounted to, but I knew I wanted them to thrive. I would set about developing their colony and improving their quality of life. I would cultivate their population.

I never mentioned the moles to Betsy or Rick and they never visited that part of the yard. Ever. At night they would come home and we would sit together on their porch and they would sip wine and, I think, try to cheer me up and distract me with jokes and stories, complaints about work and politics and family and things.

They told me my spirit seemed to be improving, but they were in the dark about the molehill so they probably just assumed any improvements in my demeanor were a result of their positive influence on my spirit, or the fresh country air, or something as simple as a physical separation from my problems. Little did they know, I was purchasing earthworms from the bait shop each morning and saturating the molehill with food. I picked weeds and gathered stones from the perimeter of their lump in order that the mound and the tunnels underneath might grow. I cleared the upturned soil around each hole so that the dirt pile looked like a big brown belly covered with tiny navels. I spent hours on a little throne I had fashioned from soil, basking in the loving presence of the labor.

And I began to heal.

And the colony began to prosper. I was discovering new holes each day, which meant new tunnels. They were building. I was proud. The worms were wriggling about everywhere as well, multiplying for the moles to eat. I felt a little bad about feeding the worms to the moles, but I chalked it up to a natural order. Besides, I liked the moles better. So I kept buying worms.

When I saw Shelley was calling again - Shelley was my girlfriend or ex-girlfriend or something like that - I didn't pick up my phone. I was sitting on the molehill late in the afternoon and my phone began to vibrate. I was surprised to have it in my pocket. I hadn't received a phone call in weeks. In some ways, I had begun to forget about the outside world completely. When I looked at the screen and saw who was calling, my heart got weak and fluttery but just then, as if on cue, a furry little head poked out of the dirt near my foot and smiled at me. I put the phone away. I was startled by my reaction. I hadn't expected to be smiling back.

Continuing with my initiative to develop the mole colony, I thought I might like to introduce a new species of mole to the labor. I thought it would be nice to diversify the population. It had seemed to work pretty well with humans, right? I knew I would have to go to a lot of trouble catching them on my own, so I sought out a store that sold exotic pets.

I borrowed Betsy's truck and drove there. I bought two-dozen moles: twelve boars and twelve sows. The clerk was a kid with pimples and a lisp. He assured me, with what I took for undue relish, that this particular species of mole mated aggressively and was very fertile. I would grow the population in no time. And then the tunnels would spread.

It was springtime and Betsy began to plant. Her garden was not near the labor. Like I said, she never went near there. Ever.

I would help her plant things on the weekends. Flowers and vegetables and carnivorous plants to keep away the mosquitoes and flies. It was good for me to help her and I felt like I was starting to earn my keep even though I probably wasn't. I wasn't very good at gardening. I had lived in the city my whole life.

The tunnels were spreading. I began to notice new holes in the lawn on my way to and from the mound each day. The new species that I had introduced were larger and more skittish around me, but they seemed to be excellent diggers. The holes were popping up closer and closer to the cabin and the garden around it. I wanted to encourage the moles to build in the other direction, toward the woods, but I had no idea how to go about accomplishing it. I thought and thought but nothing came. Still, I fed them worms. And under my care, the labor continued to grow.

Betsy was an experienced gardener, so when her young plants started to die and the grass began to recede from the area around her garden, she suspected moles right way. She asked me to help her get rid of them. For days, she searched on her hands and knees through the grass, finding new holes like hidden Easter eggs all over the lawn, but still she refused to go near the mound. If she had, she would have discovered a finely manicured little hill, swollen on the inside with moles. And one small dirt throne on top.

Rick was a carpenter by trade, but he was also a volunteer firefighter. He had access to high-pressured hoses. He and Betsy decided to use those hoses to flood the moles' tunnel system. I didn't know what to say to them, so I didn't say anything.

The night before Rick was to bring the fire truck by the cabin, I slipped away from my futon and went out into the yard. It was pitch black out in the country at night. I had never really gotten used to not having noise and lights around me after dark, and until that night I had rarely strayed more than a few feet from the cabin's front porch after dusk. This time I went all the way to the mole-hill, walking on tiptoes to avoid any invisible moles at my feet that might've popped out to gaze at the stars or take in a bit of fresh air.

I sat on the mound and addressed the moles in a loud whisper. I was sure most of them were too far underground to hear, and probably sleeping, but I did it anyway. I had to get this off my chest. Also, I had been drinking again, for the first time since I came to the cabin.

"Listen, Moles. I am afraid I may have steered you wrong. You have been the best thing that has happened to me in a long time, maybe too long, longer than I even remember. And I have tried my best for you…you know I have, don't you? But I've failed you. I was over…zealous, my intensity was over…wrought. And now you all may die. You must move your labor into the woods. Tonight. Find a new home. And live there. Thrive."

By now I was lying prostrate on the dirt pile, whispering into one of the larger holes. I could hear my voice as if it were someone else's. I sounded like a man singing through a thick wet pillow. I felt ridiculous. I went back inside. That night I had a dream about underwater caverns. The fish inside had fur. And tails. They were moles, I think.

The next day, two small fire trucks rolled up with three or four volunteer firemen in t-shirts and ballcaps. I had already helped Betsy situate both of the cabin's garden hoses in the holes closest to the house. The water did little more than trickle out, with only slight damage to the vast system of tunnels.

I sat on the porch with a lemonade and tried to enjoy myself. I was failing at it.

There were four fire hoses, all totaled. I watched from the porch as the men dug out the holes to make room for the heavy steel nozzles at the end of each hose. I closed my eyes as they turned on the pumps.

I could hear the water moving through the hoses. It sounded like what I imagined the innards of a waterpark might sound like. And then there were screams.

Betsy was shrill like a bird when she screamed. Rick and the firemen sounded shocked. Someone began laughing. But what yanked my heart into my chest was the blast of tiny squeals, almost a song like birds in a tree. Hundreds of moles. Screaming.

I opened my eyes. Water seeped out through the lawn everywhere I looked. But that's not what was causing all the commotion.

The mound in the back corner of the yard had turned into a fantastic fountain with streams of high-pressured water spraying everywhere. Each stream started and stopped in a sporadic way. All these tiny black clumps were being shot into the air. I noticed that as many of the clumps landed, they scurried off into the woods. Some didn't. I could tell it was time for me to go back to the city.

After about twenty minutes of watching the yard leak and flush like a toilet, Betsy, Rick, the firemen, and I were all standing around what used to be the mound. The hoses had been turned off. The hill had been blown apart at the sides. You could see in some places where the animals' passages had been. To my surprise, the top of the mound was in relatively decent shape. Muddy and misshapen but still intact.

One of Rick's firemen buddies was the first to speak. "Looks almost like a little throne," he chuckled, pointing. "Looks like the moles had a king."

We all nodded in agreement.

Then I spoke up. "Had one," I said.

And everyone just laughed.

Hummingbirds

We have been staying at my mother's house. She is going through a late life-divorce after thirty-fuve years of marriage to my father. The house is empty and over-sized for one woman. The ceilings are disappearing and the local flora has begun to creep in the windows and sprout roots on the wall. Black spiders that remind you of pubic hair have claimed the downstairs bathroom, where they feast and pogo from wall to mirror like children on too much juice.

"I'm old," my mother says. "My family has moved on and now I'm all alone." We have moved out here temporarily to keep her company. We have moved out here to show her kindness. We have moved out here to watch her around alcohol and sharp things.

We sleep on the same couch I slept on during high school. We battle wisteria and hack through cobwebs with field hockey sticks. We fall headfirst into photo albums. We discover empty rooms and transform them into art studios. We drink wine from graying bottles. We attract a party of small creatures to the yard with a cylinder of sunflower seeds, then we offer them a bath. We bought my mother a hummingbird feeder and fill it with blood-red syrup, but no hummingbirds come to visit. We hold séances for them one afternoon, then give up. We watch premium cable. But mostly we eat.

We eat obscure cheeses spread with foreign condiments. We stir-fry pea pods and elfin ears of corn. I burn meat on what was my father's grill. We order pizza. We eat licorice shoelaces and wayward mosquitoes, but mostly we eat sweets. We scarf cannolis. We munch crullers. We visit the snowball stand in bare feet and sleep next to pitchers of lemonade. We grow fat on melancholy pastries. We sweat sugar in the sun. We speak, through a saccharine haze, of taking our vitamins. We speak in past tense of the future as if it were part of a childhood dream.

"Five more minutes!?" you plead when you hear me rustling awake around noon. I wake up each day with things stuck to me. Scraps of paper, candy wrappers, mosquito bites. One of my eyes is sealed closed with sleep. I follow your voice. I find you on the back porch, naked except for a boy's bathing suit I haven't seen since I learned to swim. You're on a beach towel, ecstatic near the magnolia tree. Your back is arched. Your lips and toes are curled like seahorse tails and the low sky flutters with colors. I have to rub my eyes. I have to peel my one eye open.

Thousands of tiny birds beat the humid air around you like insects. They attack you with beaks like needles, sliding wire-tongues in and out of your pores. The humming birds grow fat and heavy on your blood sugar. A rainbow of hovering ulcers.

The wet air smells like honeysuckle. A candy factory. The neighbors' dogs are barking. "Five more minutes," you groan and I head back inside for a soda. When I come back you've turned into a raisin, which will make my mother feel young at supper this evening. I thank you for that.

Everything Is Fine

Hi. I think I may have found something that belongs to you. Did you post a flyer – a bunch of them - with this phone number on it, advertising a reward for a missing tortoise? Anyway, I think I have him. Or her or whatever. I'm not sure how to figure out the sex. And I respect your turtle's privacy too much to ask.

I want you to know everything is fine.

I saw your address at the bottom of the flyer. I'm two neighborhoods over. I found him in front of my house.

He must've travelled at least fifteen blocks to get here! You probably don't think that's funny. I was impressed though.

He was on his back in the sun the afternoon I found him. I imagine a dog tipped him over with his nose. Or maybe some kids did it and left him there. He was fine though, except for being upside down. He was kicking his legs at the sky. It was like he was trying to swim through the clouds. I knew he was your turtle. I had just seen the flyer on my walk home from the bar.

I never find anything, by the way. Not even lucky pennies. It's like I walk around all day looking at stuff and everything good is invisible.

I flipped him over and he looked confused, like he had forgotten how the world looks rightside-up. I know the feeling. I let him get used to everything. Then I went super slow up the walk to my porch, kind of looking back over my shoulder to see if he would follow me. He didn't. So I just picked him up and brought him inside.

That was yesterday.

I fed him spinach leaves. They were a topping on a pizza in my fridge. The pizza was only a day old. The leaves were still okay. He liked it. Then I took my shirt off and lay down on the floor and sat him on my chest. The bottom of his shell was cold at first, but we were there a while and I got used to it. Then it felt good. I think we were both very tired.

When I woke up it was dark. He was still on my chest, looking at me. I haven't woken up to someone looking at me for a long time. It was nice to have a pair of eyes there, knowing I was asleep. This morning I gave him a bath. At first I did it because I wanted him to look nice for you when you came to pick him up. I used warm water and soft soap and my fingers. He's so wrinkly! I needed a Q-tip for the really tight places. I thought he would struggle against me, but he didn't. I've never had a pet that didn't struggle. He extended his neck so I could wipe his head and the soft area behind it.

I put him in a box and headed toward the bar to get your number off the flyer. I promise I was going to give him back. I saved the number in my phone. I thought about holding onto him for a couple of days, just until it felt like we didn't need each other so much, then calling. Then I felt bad when I thought of all those flyers you made. You must've been really worried.

So I guess I'm just calling now to tell you that everything is fine. I promise I was going to give him back.

The Job You Quit Can Be Your Own

Shepherds circled their flock in bumper cars on the farm where I grew up, then old. I was the one who used my foot to push them free when they got stuck. I was the shepherd's shepherd. The sky was an electric cage.

In the warm months, the sheep were shorn for cotton candy and in the cold months they were slaughtered. We ate gyro meat on sticks around a campfire when the dinner bell clanged. I cried wolf but no one ever heard me beneath the carousel's organ music, piped into our ear canals through glass soda bottles. I chanted it like a spell.

Wolf, I said. Wolf, again. Wolf. Wolf.

The farm was in a valley and the sheep grazed on the foothills nearby. They ate dandelions and chewed on plastic straws. The mountains on either side were crawling with rollercoasters. Most of the rollercoasters were named after rattlesnakes. Just one machine was named for the wolf but it was old, seen as something only for children to ride.

I never rode any of them. I wanted to be helpful, not upside down. I spent most of my time at my post or wandering, on patrol whenever the cage was busted. You can always count on someone to be stuck somewhere, I told whoever would listen, if you look for them to be. It is convincing others they need your push that proves difficult. People laughed at me, their faces turned up at the moon. Wolf, I whispered in the dining hall. Wolf, I said to a cow.

If it was true the wolves no longer existed, I would miss them. In their absence, the plantation had turned into a carnival.

The Spider's Eggs

I woke up after the storm and went outside to see what had been broken. The deck was intact, but all around the trees were crushed like bad teeth. My eye was drawn to the center of the grey deck where, above the strewn pine needles and sticks, just inches over a composite-wood plank, there was floating a small round white thing. A puff. What looked like part of a piece of popcorn. My girlfriend and I had not eaten popcorn last night, before the storm, after, or during. We watched a movie, but we didn't eat popcorn.

Yet there it was, hovering. A tiny dove on a plateau of wind. I watched it until I was covered with dew, then I turned on a sprinkler. The hose had been punctured and was leaking out the side. The spray was weak. It mocked the rainstorm. The stream barely moved the floating piece of popcorn. I pulled the hose closer, but the popcorn barely shook, suspended in mid-air against the water.

I decided the puff was not a piece of popcorn but a spider's egg. After all, it was hanging from a spider's web. I wondered how many fetal spiders were in there. It was so tiny. What I remembered from storybooks and nature shows was that spiders gave birth to thousands of babies. There were thousands of lives inside that tiny dangling puff. I didn't want so many spiders around my dead mother's house, which I was fixing up and eventually trying to sell, get rid of once and for all.

I held the hose right up close to the egg. Point blank. I blasted it. Then I rubbed the wet egg into the deck with my foot.

I spent the rest of the day cleaning up after the storm. Just the deck not the world around it, which remained broken. For that, I would call the insurance company. By the time I was able to sleep, the deck was as clean and grey as it had ever been.

The next morning I woke up and went outside for a cigarette. The egg was still there. It was dangling like an angel, from a nearly invisible thread the same as before. It was like it had never moved. It was also like I had never killed all those spiders. Like I had been given a second chance.

I was tempted to wake my girlfriend up but I hadn't told her about yesterday's egg. I knew she would be unimpressed. I was alone with the egg and that felt nice. I peered even closer this time, so close it was almost touching my eyeball. I considered not crushing it this time around.

But I did it anyway. I didn't want the house to have any more spiders than it already did. We already had a lot of spiders.

The next day the porch was empty of floating eggs. I imagined a mother spider broken inside, weeping out of many eyes, tucked somewhere in the tree above me. I wished she would just move on.

The Maids Make Me Uncomfortable (In High-Grade Silk)

The cobweb mavens are restless, searching for a magnifying glass. Without it, you say, they will be lost. You and I are seated at the counter. There is one dirty spoon in the sink. You grind your teeth like gears. You eat teeth. Some people believe they can't swim, you say. They spend their whole lives dry, but never drying off. But humans do float, you assure me. You ask me for a shovel, when you really mean a spoon. I am scared to move, lest I break the silky thread woven between us.

And the cobweb mavens turn the apartment upside down before our eyes like a magic parlor trick. From here the view looks different. The cushions are in disarray and the wastebasket has been spilled on the carpet. Flowers wilt too rapidly. Smoke seems to drip from the speakers. We see the crumbs of our life all over the place like bits of meat on a pizza. It bothers us. We go on pretending to be busy. All the while a chubby spider hunches in the corner, grinning.

Signatures in Dust
(Deep Empty Wells of Information)

There are no pamphlets for moving back into your dead family's house. There are probably ones on bereavement and mourning dead family members, but the members of my family are all still alive. It is only the family itself that is dead. The members have scattered themselves over the country like ashes. There are no pamphlets about how to get their smell from the property in order to make a sale. There is plenty of information about removing odors, but not the particular tang I am looking to be rid of in the end. In fact, none of them mention my family at all. There is also nothing online about cupboards that might be haunted or at least won't close all the way and sometimes pop open in your face like they are trying to slap you. There is nothing online about the horrible size of empty rooms or what to do if you encounter a stuffed animal in the closet.

Do you call someone who used to be part of the family? Do you ask them if they care?

I write my name in cursive grooves through the dust on the hardwood floor in what used to be our family room. I would sit in there as a boy, on a Persian rug, and do my homework while my father's record player fizzed out bits of music that made me feel part of a larger, grown-up world. I didn't want to be a part of anything other than what I already was a part of at home.

The room is empty now. There is no rug, so I can write my name as big as I want. My name looks good enormous, dominating the family room like that. I go into other rooms to look for more dust. I write my name in those rooms too. My mood begins to lift. When I am finished I have to walk on the tips of my toes to avoid messing up my signatures, which are perfect. They bring the house together. I imagine writing my own pamphlet that would teach people to perform this activity and others like it themselves. I would have nothing to tell them about the odor though. The only way to get rid of the odor is to stop breathing.

Hunting Water Bears

Tardigrades could have taken over the world, I thought. And we wouldn't even know it.

I learned about tardigrades from the Internet on a sad winter morning in my apartment. They were microscopic segmented animals with eight legs and tiny feet. Their feet were supposed to look like bear claws. That's why they were also called water bears. Water bears were plump and they ambled like a bear too, which was why some scientists thought they were cute.

Sometimes when I felt lonely or disconnected, I needed to think about animals. I felt like they knew something I didn't and if I thought about them I could learn a piece of it. After awhile I would get distracted by the world and forget the other animals were even a part of it, much less keepers of life's secrets.

I was admiring water bears on my computer. At first they were horrific, photographed under the microscope like space parasites. In fact, scientists have launched them into space. They lived. They have been the only animals that were able to do this, according to the Internet. I wondered how many animals had been launched.

Water bears were tough, the Internet said, in extreme heat, cold or pressure. They could extend their life to over 120 years by hunkering down in a tiny shell like a cuticle, to reverse their metabolism. They shut down all of their body's processes and go into a hibernation that resembles death, only to wake up later under different circumstances. I had often wanted to do that. Sleep through the bad times and wake up to epiphany.

After awhile I understood why people found them cute, even if they didn't have any eyes.

Water bears lived all over the world, even tall mountains and deep-sea trenches. I put on clothes and went out to find some. I will take them home, I thought, and we will share my apartment. They won't be my pets. We will just live together.

I didn't have a microscope or slides. Out on the sidewalk I realized I would probably need a microscope if I wanted to see anything, but the hunt felt too important to just give up on because of a missing tool. I wanted to keep feeling like something was important to me.

There was a park not far from my house, near the art museum. Water bears liked moss and other wet areas. I figured the park was a good place for moss.

I had been walking everywhere in alleys, to avoid running into people. This time I walked on the street like a normal person.

It rained a little on my way to the park. I was cold but things were okay, better than normal in fact, because I had a purpose.

A water bear could survive in any temperature. I thought the rain would make them more active. I imagined living with a tiny animal that had been asleep since before I was born. I pictured myself talking to him beneath the lamp next to my bed. Nodding as if he said something very intelligent in response.

The park was a popular place to walk dogs. I didn't go there very often because I didn't have a dog. I lived alone. My ex-girlfriend used to live with me and she had always wanted a dog. I thought we weren't responsible enough. Whenever we walked anywhere, she had to stop and pet every dog we passed. I didn't understand it then, but now I realize it was just her way of trying to feel connected. It was her version of thinking about animals.

I wonder why I have not mentioned my girlfriend earlier. It is maybe because she was no longer my girlfriend, but I doubt that is why it has never stopped me before. I had been trying not to think about her. I had been trying to think about bigger things, smaller things, life, things like tardigrades.

I was thinking about all these things and not about where I was walking, not about where my feet were hitting the earth, when I stepped in dogshit. I didn't know that I had stepped in dogshit at first, but I would later find out I had stepped in a fresh pile of wet green muck. I just walked around with the odor in my nostrils, looking for water bears, and thinking the world smelled like shit. Trying to pretend it was beautiful.

I was at the bottom of a stone staircase, near the outhouses and the fence behind the museum's sculpture garden. I was scooping moss into a plastic bag. There was dogshit on my shoe and smeared up my dirty white sock, but I still didn't know it. There was dogshit on the cuff of my pants too. When I squatted down to scoop up the moss (and hopefully water bears), my thigh touched my heel and it all spread up the back of my pants. I was marked with shit and scooping wet moss into a plastic bag. In my head, I imagined people who walked past might think I am a scientist, or at least an artist collecting materials. I would have settle for being an artist.

The tardigrades are waking up in there, I thought. I was holding a bag full of tiny resurrections.

73

I headed back toward the house. As I walked past the sculpture garden, I saw a girl in a blue puffball hat. She looked like my ex-girlfriend and was walking a dog. At first I thought it was her and I panicked because she was right in front of me and there was no escape. Then we made eye contact for a second and I saw it was not her, but a stranger. I had already started to wave though, I guess in an attempt to seem natural. The girl's dog pulled ahead of her. He was thrilled to see me and began licking my leg like it was covered in honey. The girl made a face like I was a giant boil that had just exploded and her dog was now feasting on. She pulled the dog off me and hurried away, kind of squeaking. That was when I looked down and realized I had gotten myself covered in shit. I sniffed the air, like I was trying to make sure I had the right odor. It was unmistakable. The shit was dark green and wet and didn't look all that different from the moss I was carrying around with me in a plastic bag. I put my head down and made for the alleys.

As I was walking, almost scurrying, with my sack of moss and (hopefully) tardigrades held close, I began to think about soil, dirt, the earth itself. I wondered how much of it was made of excrement.

A lot of it, I imagined. Maybe all of it contains some kind of excrement, I thought, from some bug or bird or bacteria. I decided to look this up online after I got home and cleaned myself up.

I thought about all the possible pieces of earth my foot could have landed on. I have small feet. How many of those small foot-shaped spots contained water bears? How many contained excrement particles? How much was just gravel or rock? And how many were piles of hot green sludge at the end of a recent pass through the body of dog?

The whole world felt unlikely. Why should I step anywhere, let alone in this one place where a dog just relieved itself? I was linked to the dog and whatever animal it had eaten and whatever that animal had eaten and plants and soil and more excrement and so on.

Somehow it was this thought that did it, not the microscopic animals in my baggy or anything I learned on the Internet that day. It was this thought about landing in fresh shit instead of landing in nothing that made me feel reconnected. I considered getting a dog. I considered getting ten dogs.

Chalkdust

I found a very tiny sneaker on the sidewalk outside our doorstep today. The canvas tongue was grey as the bruised sky overhead. The sides had pale blue stripes that brought to mind the veins on an infant's arm. Instead of going to work, I went back inside to find a thick stick of pink chalk from among the other trash that filled the room that should have belonged to our daughter. When I came back out, the sun was shining through a broken cloud. I drew a pink circle around the lonely shoe. My neighbor was outside, waiting for the bus. I asked him where the shoe had come from. "Fell out of the sky, I guess." He smiled at me, then wandered down to the next stop.

I couldn't go anywhere. Time had frozen, with me inside.

Bees in the City

Bees in the City find flowers. I have not noticed anything beautiful in weeks. I think this while sitting on my stoop. These are the dull humid days that cause fungal infections and people to fall off their roofs.

I stare at a vacant parking lot, wishing a flower would grow. Right in front of me, as I sit.

Bees find flowers, I think. An animal the size of a cashew, with a brain the size of a sesame seed, discovers all the tiny flowers hidden in cracked sidewalks and sky-rise flowerboxes around town. "Unlikely" is the only word I can find.

I look around and all I see is concrete and traffic and people, sometimes with dogs. I imagine that dogs smell flowers, although I don't think they seek them out. Dogs don't eat flowers.

I don't either, but I plan to look for them anyway.

When I get off my stoop, my thoughts have left me buzzing, alert. The flowers will find me, I pray to no one in particular.

Ruins

I went on vacation to the Far East with a tour group made up of my small family and a large white cruise ship of people whose faces I had trouble seeing. Some of them were families themselves, others not, merely couples or satellites, all of them chattering or yawning as they returned for seconds and thirds at the buffet or waterslide or slot machines. Time moved slowly because they were constantly freezing it with their cameras. I stayed in the cabin as much as I could, guarding myself - even from my family - with a shiny paperback plus the lies of seasickness and exhaustion that collected on my tongue as easily as saliva. It wasn't much different than my existence at home or work. I was afraid of everything and had been my whole life, but only slightly. Not enough to do anything about it. Mostly I was afraid of people, all people, because they reminded me of myself.

We loaded into busses lined up near docks stained with dried salt that cooked in the sun. A man who looked like he didn't have any eyeballs drove us to a long-devastated holy site located up steep cobbled stairways carved into the side of a mountain that looked like a pile of boiled dishrags. Most of the tour group stayed at the bottom, where there were merchants and children selling umbrellas even though it was sunny, monkeys that squeaked like dolls and posed for the photographs everyone was taking. I had the energy of a continental breakfast coursing through my veins and charged up ahead of my family and everyone else like I had done as a boy when my parents took me hiking in the low, dull mountains that line the western part of our little state back home.

At the top of the path, there was an opening in front of a cavern door. On the other side of the opening was a high cliff that looked over a purple horizon. At the edge of the cliff, staring out, was a tiny man, ancient and shrunken by the weight of time, with a small hat like a teacup and a long moustache down to his ankles that struck me as exactly the type of facial feature a caterpillar might develop in old age. I went over to stand next to him. I hoped he had some water or something with electrolytes. For some reason, I didn't mind asking him for it. In most cases, there was a painful sense of looming disaster when I had to ask something of a stranger, no matter how mundane the request. I stood next to the tiny man like an elf, and towered over him. I felt like part of the mountain, the peak. Before I even had a chance to introduce myself, the wise man began to speak.

"Ruin your reputation," he whispered in a voice that reminded me of an emergency radio transmission. "Then you will live quite freely."

He was right. I had been pent up my whole life come to think of it, first in the suburbs then in the city then in the suburbs again, now on this vacation. The pressure of being a human with other humans trying our best to act human in a better-than-human kind of way was like trying to hold in gas.

It was settled. I would quit my job in an embarrassing way possibly involving a mass e-mail, dress in pajamas and slippers, grow a layer of fungus on my belly, ride a dirt bike on the street, eat crayfish from the neighbors' prayer fountain, build a burial mound in my backyard, chase seagulls, sleep on sidewalks, sleep with dogs, live in a highway median strip, live underwater, drink gin in the morning and stay sober at night, let my lawn go, wear multiple plaids, get a facial tattoo, pick a fight, run from a fight, tell people I love them, tell people I don't, shave my head to feel the wind, grow toenails like claws, spend fortunes on lottery tickets and chocolate cake, steal things I don't want, get arrested, go to jail, get raped, enjoy it, get kicked out of jail, climb a mountain like this one in order to get to heaven, stomp the mountain into a pit of lava when I reach the summit, ask heaven to come to me, learn to fly, tell God I don't exist, talk to strangers and like it, feel free.

I looked down at the man, not on him because I had developed a great respect for him as I stood there contemplating his advice. His head was about the size of a baseball, I thought, and just as round. I pet him gently near his brain as a way to say thank you, then let my hand linger before I gave him a little push. His legs trailed behind that round head like streamers as he dove into the ravine.

I was not quite ready for all the freedom he preached. I wasn't sure that anyone else was either. And I could hear them coming.

Biker Queen Fishing Story

My neighbor dragged me fishing, like bait. He wanted me to do business with his "best buddy," an attorney out west where I maybe wanted some land. I didn't know what I wanted. The guy was a Mormon or something. The whole thing was weird. I didn't get to know him. But I could tell he had problems. We all have problems.

And it turns out fishing was mostly waiting and drinking, which was pretty much what I expected but worse. I would've given a fortune to have ants injected in my veins, if only for the excitement. The only thrill on the water was an emasculated ranger threatening a group of teens that were throwing themselves off a cliff like members of a suicide cult.

When we were done trying to fool the fishes, I insisted we have another drink before the long ride back home. Part of me hoped I would pass out before then and they would just tuck me into the backseat of my neighbor's SUV and wake me when we were in my driveway. My neighbor and his buddy were reluctant but they finally agreed to stop at a bar & grill near the reservoir.

The parking lot, bar, patio, and surrounding territory was full of bikers and their girlfriends. It was a rally! They all looked like they were having a great time. Like they had been having a great time all day. A much better time than we'd had sitting out on that mud-filled lake.

At the bar, I drank a lot - very quickly it felt like. It's hard to tell. The sun had been so hot out there; I was in a daze. I told my companions I was stumbling because of the rocking of the boat on the reservoir, which was basically the City's glass of water and no choppier than a puddle.

I admired the bikers. They didn't have to go home to their nagging wives or dull girlfriends; their fun wives and party-hearty girlfriends were right here with them, egging them on. Hitting the open road. Grilling chunks of dinosaur meat. Dancing to loud rock 'n' roll music. But mostly drinking outside on picnic tables.

The prettiest of the girls at the rally was barely 18. Her lips were like raspberries about to spoil. I disgusted myself just thinking about her. I have two daughters. One of them is dead. The other is all grown up. We're all all grown up.

I wasn't interested in raspberry-lipped infants. I wanted to meet a real woman. A woman my age. A woman I could have conceivably married years ago if we both had lived different lives. I ordered a large steak and another shot - my second and the food hadn't even come yet, my neighbor pointed out.

"I need it," I told him, and mumbled something about "sea legs."

I scanned the party like a sailor desperate for the temptations of a harbor town. My neighbor's buddy, the attorney, noticed me.

"Watcha lookin' for?" I don't mean to write him so hickish, but that's the closest I can get to what he sounded like on paper.

I sound like water being sucked down a drain. Why fight it?

"I'm searching out the Biker Queen," I said. "The Matriarch."

I looked deeper into the party. A mass appeared on the horizon. Flesh. And leather. Smoke. I hopped up from the table.

I'd found her.

She was holding court in back.

She was not the oldest at the bar, but she was close to it and she was by dog shits the meanest-looking. The alpha female. That's what I was looking for. I wondered for a second if she had gotten her status from being the alpha male's woman, but I pushed the thought from my head and with tipsy aplomb sort of danced in her direction, too drunk to be embarrassed about my Hawaiian shirt. A gift from my wife's awful mother.

The Biker Queen was about twelve-foot-tall it looked and as wide as a tank. Motorcycles zipped around her like flies around a record-breaking bovine turd. The sexy old hag had long hair, black and white like the movies. Young blonde wet tee shirt contest losers clung to her Viking braids like burrs in a golden retriever's mane. Her tattoos were ancient runes and vomiting bald eagles, battleships straddled by the Grim Reaper, swastikas dining on elves' blood. She wore a crown of barbed wire and a ripped tank top that read: "I don't need a helmet, YOU DO!" If I'd had better judgment or wasn't so dissatisfied with my life, I would've worn one to approach her.

I pushed across the tented dance floor and covered myself with biker sweat in the process. At the far end she sat on two oversized picnic tables, flanked by a pair of salivating gray wolves. Heat radiated from her leather pants and nearly blew me back to my table where I was supposed to be waiting for a shitty steak I didn't even want. I was supposed to be back there dreading the prospect more than death of the long drive back with my neighbor and his Mormon (?) to see my wife, a wife who felt more like a genetic condition than someone who wanted to share her fleeting time on Earth with me. The feeling was mutual. I fought through the crowd, still dancing, now holding two light beers.

When I got up close, the Biker Queen turned out to be three times as big as she had looked from across the dance floor. I had to borrow a microphone from the deejay who was too busy bonging beers and blowing the foam out on bare tits in the crowd to notice. I could only imagine what my neighbor was thinking.

"Hello!" I screamed, tugging on one of her leg hairs. Boy, was I feeling ballsy. "I am a lonely fisherman!"

"Did I hear something?" Tables turned over when she spoke.

"YES! You heard ME! A lonely fisherman who hates to fish and is dissatisfied with his current and longtime situation in life!"

She saw me now and scooped me up in her palm, brought me close to eye level.

"Little Man," she said. She scratched me on my bald, sun-burned head with one of her spiky rings. "You do not look like a fisherman."

"Well, thanks," I said. "I'm not really."

"You look like a fish. You don't even look like a fish. You look like a tadpole, blind to the murky world around you."

"That's true!" I said. It was hard not to agree with her. "I loved my life at one time! But I was only a little boy and many years have passed since then. Now I am old and blind! And bored and boring! Marry me!"

The Biker Queen laughed so loud that for a second I was afraid her mate would hear and come stomping through the forest from wherever he was and skin me, then use my bones as toothpicks. But I was too caught up in the moment to give fear a chance.

"So . . . is that a no?" I asked.

"No!" she roared. I nearly fell off her hand. "That's a YES! Take me home and bed me now or regret this moment and the rest of your life forever!"

If this had been a cartoon and not real life, I would've gulped or at least said, "Gulp."

Instead I said, "Fuck."

This is why I said, "Fuck." I love my wife. In fact, after twenty-five years, it would be impossible to love myself, or even tolerate myself, without loving my wife. I know that. And I know I am afraid to be anything but plainly unhappy because I don't know how. I would rather be comfortable than change. If the grass is green, it turns brown when I get near it.

What I didn't know was how to marry a biker queen, let alone have sex with one, or live in her sidecar and make her happy. I wanted to though. Or, part of me did. I wanted to crawl in her earlobe and build a nest, hoist my pirate flag and sleep on a bed of golden wax with the sound of engines roaring and the wild country whipping past like outside an open freight car. Not because I loved her, but because I hated what I had become.

"Are you okay, Little Man?"

"I'm not sure." I had to admit it.

All she did was laugh, long and slow, careful not to let me fall even though the earth was shaking.

"Could you give me a ride home?" I asked. "I can't stand the guys I came here with."

"You don't have to marry me, Little Man." Her smile let me know life would continue whether I had anything to do with it or not. And everything was back to normal again. Until her husband rolled up on top of an enormous dust cloud, followed by what looked like some lost tribe of Neanderthal warriors. Then I truly wished that I had not gone fishing but had stayed at home where I belong.

Lullaby

White tigers with red stripes like peppermints prowl the tall grass in the vacant lot at the end of our block. The children sing to them. It keeps the tigers from escaping. But none of us are fooled. They will never be tame. So we let the children keep singing, even though our ears are sensitive.

The birds in our neighborhood are jealous of the clouds because they fly without effort and never need to search for food. The birds are thinking, "Why must we be all the time pecking and hoarding for the winter?" I can see it in their little black eyes.

The cracks in the sidewalk grow purple weeds. The homeless hold séances in the alley. They are trying to levitate the neighborhood. We can hear their cries at night and smell the things they are burning. We can hear the children cooing softly to the tigers. We can smell the weeds. On the roof are night birds who grumble at the sky even though the clouds are invisible.

Old people don't open the fire hydrants in the summer anymore. We let the children do that, provided that they take turns cooling off so there will always be at least one of them singing. We tell ourselves quiet lies to keep cool. We don't trust anyone anymore. We don't even trust our bodies.

The children have a game they play with scissors. It's sort of like tag, only bloodier. They chase around the gushing hydrant trying to cut each other's hair. My hair fell out years ago. I kept it and put it in a jar, but it disintegrated.

My hair turned to dust in a jar.

I watch things from my window. It is on the fourth floor, where I live with the soul of my dead wife. Her name was Bereniece. Her soul doesn't have a name though. Souls don't have names. The things I watch mostly have names. Some of them don't. Like the children's game, that doesn't have a name. If something doesn't have a name, I could give it one. But I don't. I don't like naming things. It's not for me. I like describing things better.

The streets in our neighborhood are made out of drugs. If you lick them, you will get high. There are lots of people with brown tongues around here. But they are still good people inside. Even if they are out there licking the street to get high. We are all fragile until we die. The minute we die, we grow tough. It's easy then. Life is the hardest thing to trust.

It's nice to have neighbors if they are friendly. Even if they are not, you can still watch them out the window.

Nobody remembers exactly how the tigers got here. "It used to be a different neighborhood," everybody says, although no one is clear on the dates.

Legend has it that when a tiger dies, the other tigers eat its skin then bury the bones in the grass. It's only a legend though. No one has seen a tiger die. Except for maybe the children. And they aren't talking.

The children grow older and older without visibly aging. Or

else new children replace them each year. It's hard to tell. I have been watching them a long time and it has become less and less clear all the while. I often find myself repeating things.

There is ivy on the side of my building. One year the Super, a fat man named Bob, let it get out of control. The vines began to climb over the window, spreading like fingers on a hand trying to block out my view. I never opened my window in those days, so it was easy for ivy to grow right over. I called Bob. He promised he would fix it. Told me not to try getting out on the ledge. It was too high up and I would fall to my death. I told him okay but to hurry. I needed to be able to see out my window.

Bob didn't come for three days and when he did, he only took a look at the problem and said he'd need to come back with a very large ladder; it was too dangerous out there on the ledge without one. I asked him if he owned a ladder that tall.

"I used to," he said, as if that were some kind of help. He said his cousin Bill might have one in storage somewhere. He said he would talk to Bill. "If he'll let me on his property," Bob said.

This wasn't providing me with much hope, but Bob said to hang in there. He would have the ivy off soon. I went mad for six days in my apartment. My skin began to blister and peel. Around my toes and my armpits. I thought I was rotting. Some kind of vitamin d deficiency, I figured. Or maybe a fungal infection. I don't know. I'm not a doctor.

I had had enough waiting. I was resolved to fix the problem myself. Remove obtrusive vegetation and let the sunlight fill my apartment along with the sights and sounds of the neighborhood around me. I find it is important to be aware of your surroundings. We are surrounded at all times.

I don't own garden shears or anything because I live in a studio apartment with no outdoor space. Besides, I was too old for gardening. This happened to be an emergency and therefore an exception. I took a Swiss Army knife out with me instead.

The ivy was like a green waterfall coming down over the window. My apartment was a secret cave. I managed to push the window open some, stretching the ivy just enough to slide my slender frame out the window and through the leafy cascade.

My ankle got wrapped. The leather laces on my slipper were caught. I tried to free it but I can't bend like I used to and my balance was never impressive. I was trapped in the tangled growth, half my body still on the windowsill and the other protruding from the ivy out onto the ledge four stories above the ground. I could hear the birds chirping on the roof above me. I could tell they were excited. I could hear the children down below me, singing. I could hear my wife's nameless soul inside the apartment, scolding me.

I tried to get my knife open. It was difficult. I didn't know whether I should use the scissors or the knife or the saw, so I tried to open them all. Besides, it was hard telling the tools apart with the knife closed so I was mostly just endied guessing anyway. It was frustrating. The tools were very hard to open. I wobbled as I struggled with it. I almost fell. I dropped the knife - which open the way it was felt something akin to holding a porcupine. I grabbed the ivy and it peeled right off the window, only hanging onto the brick by a few tiny roots. The knife fell from stories on a pigeon that was eating French fries off the sidewalk, pinning him to the mulchy interior of a tree well and killing him instantly. I had never killed an animal before. He died so I could see. I wanted to jump down on top of him, cover him up and hide him from the world. I knew that was not a healthy thought for me to have.

I sat down on my windowsill, covered in dirt with my ankle wrapped up in the ivy, and attempted to compose myself. I poked my head into the apartment and looked for Bereneice's soul. I couldn't see her. Maybe she had gone to get help. I imagined her out on the street, screaming. In tears. Begging the neighbors for help. But they wouldn't see her. They wouldn't hear. They would have to look up and see me for themselves.

I looked back outside. The neighborhood was still alive but had not noticed me. People were too concerned with licking the streets to notice danger in the sky.

A group of children had surrounded the dead bird. They were singing to it. I yelled down to them.

"Children!" I yelled. "Children! Please help me, I'm stuck! The ivy has me in its grasp!"

The children looked up at me in unison, as if going through a repeated motion in church. They stared at me, confused. They looked back down at the bird and then at me again. They were trying to make a connection.

"Please, help me!" I screamed. I had not yelled like that since before my wife had died. It felt good to yell. I felt alive too. I hadn't felt that way in at least as long. I told myself that if I lived through this, I would lick the street until it was a dirt road.

"Children!" I yelled. "I am a nice old man! I have loved you for years from this window in which I am now stuck! Please come rescue me! I know you have scissors! I have watched you playing your game! I am sorry for what happened to that bird! I didn't mean him any harm! It was only a terrible mistake!"

The homeless began to join the children below me. I could smell the incense from four stories up. They had been trying to levitate the neighborhood again. I wished they would try to levitate me. Float me like a cloud.

"Homeless people!" I yelled. "Homeless people! Please help me! I know you practice dark magic! Levitate one of the children! The one with the scissors! Float a child up here with scissors so they can cut me free!"

"We cannot levitate a child for you! Give us the security password to your front door and we will all come up and rescue you!

Children and homeless people together! Just trust us with your password!"

I had to think about this. It was a serious breach of security. Bob and my neighbors didn't want every child or homeless person coming into the building and I didn't want them coming to visit me with any regularity. I just wanted to be let back into my apartment so I could keep rotting and looking out the window with Bereneice's disapproving soul.

"I'm not sure if that's a good idea," I called down. "Maybe we could figure something else out. Like maybe you could levitate someone?"

"We cannot levitate anyone! Even if we could levitate the neighborhood, which we can't – Yet! – the levitation would include all of the streets and buildings as well so you wouldn't be any better off than you are now! In fact, if we did levitate the neighborhood it would be likely that nobody would notice! We'd just keep on living as if the neighborhood was on the ground! Give us your security code!"

"I trust you!"

I wasn't sure if I did, but I said it anyway. Sometimes the only thing left to do is trust someone.

Just then, I felt a beefy hand on my shoulder and the sound of scissors working around my tangled leg. Bob was pulling me inside. I felt like a puppet being taken off a shelf. I could hear the children and the homeless people cheering out the window. They cared about my safety. Despite what I had done to the bird. Most of the ivy had been torn off the window by my struggling and Bob's scissor-work. The light came in around torn, broken, green fingers. I could see dust floating in the light like tiny clouds and was jealous of its ability to fly. "Are you crazy, old man?" Bob asked me.

I performed a funeral service for the bird that evening.

First, I scooped him up and cleaned off the knife. He had been killed on the awl. And the corkscrew. The children and homeless people parted so I could meet my victim. Everyone stood in silence. I could hear the sound of singing in the distance, over by the vacant lot. Someone was singing to the tigers. Bird eyes look the same dead as alive, I thought. Just not moving so much. The bird looked in peace, except for the wound in his back. His little beak was part open. I could see a piece of French fry lodged in his throat.

The burial took place in a patch of dirt across from the vacant lot. I could hear the tigers rustling through the tall grass. The children were singing a lullaby. It made me very sleepy to hear. I wanted to crawl inside the tiny hole I had dug for the bird and cuddle it. Sleep inside the hole while the tigers prowled the ground above us and the children sang to keep them at bay.

I stayed away from the apartment that night. I walked the neighborhood for hours, talking to people. I licked several avenues and took part in a religious ceremony. I learned to sing. I lived out on the street among my neighbors. If the neighborhood was my home, then my apartment was only a drawer where I put things.

It only lasted that one evening though. Then I went back inside. I am old and my wife's poor soul would be worried about me. But things are better now. Now, I still spend my time by the window, but I leave it open mostly so they can hear me. I wave to people outside. And they wave back most of the time. It is the most exciting part of my day. To wave at someone and have them wave back makes me feel alive. There's nothing more fragile than being alive.

I would like to acknowledge the following publications in which many of these stories first appeared, as well as their fine editors, in no particular order: Publishing Genius, Cobalt Review, Connotation Press, Heavy Feather Review, Seltzer, Pure Slush, Artichoke Haircut, Up Literature, The Rusty Nail, Baltimore City Paper, Spilt Milk, The Cupboard, Gone Lawn, Pretend Genius, and Literary Animals, as well as my peers, faculty and the staff at University of Baltimore.

Timmy Reed is an endangered, sub-intelligent hominid from Baltimore, Maryland. Learn more at underratedanimals.wordpress.com and on Twitter @BMORETIMMYREED

The typefaces used in the design of *Tell God I Don't Exist* were Adobe Garamond Pro and Futura. No typefaces were severely injured in the making of this text.